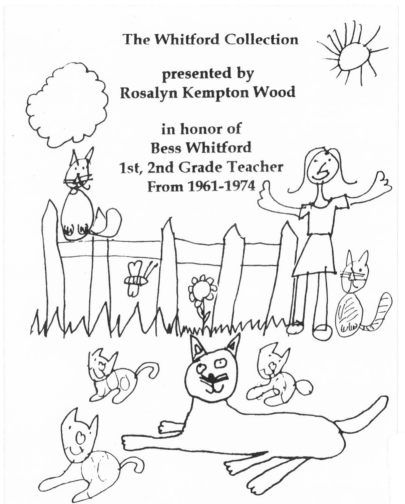

The Whitford Collection

presented by
Rosalyn Kempton Wood

in honor of
Bess Whitford
1st, 2nd Grade Teacher
From 1961-1974

Mrs. Piggle-Wiggle's Won't-Take-a-Bath Cure

ADAPTED FROM THE
MRS. PIGGLE-WIGGLE BOOKS BY

BETTY MacDONALD

ILLUSTRATED BY

BRUCE WHATLEY

HARPERCOLLINSPUBLISHERS

The Won't-Take-a-Bath-Cure
Text adapted from *Mrs. Piggle Wiggle,*
copyright 1947 by Betty MacDonald,
copyright renewed 1975 by Donald C. MacDonald
Illustrations copyright © 1997 by Bruce Whatley
Printed in the U.S.A. All rights reserved.
http://www.harperchildrens.com

Library of Congress Cataloging-in-Publication Data
MacDonald, Betty Bard.
    The won't-take-a-bath-cure / adapted from the Mrs. Piggle Wiggle books by Betty MacDonald ;
illustrated by Bruce Whatley.
        p.   cm. — (A Mrs. Piggle-Wiggle adventure)
    Summary: Mrs. Piggle-Wiggle suggests the radish cure for Patsy's bad habit of not taking a bath.
    ISBN 0-06-027630-4
    [1. Cleanliness—Fiction.   2. Baths—Fiction.   3. Radishes—Fiction.   4. Behavior—Fiction.]
I. Whatley, Bruce, ill.   II. Title.   III. Series: MacDonald, Betty Bard.   Mrs. Piggle-Wiggle adven-
ture.
PZ7.M1464Wt   1997   96-43425
[E]—dc20   CIP
                                                                                                            AC

Typography by Al Cetta
1   2   3   4   5   6   7   8   9   10
❖
First Edition

For Peter and Lisa

—B.W.

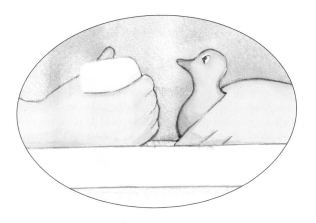

Mrs. Piggle-Wiggle lives here in our town. She has brown sparkly eyes and long brown hair, which she usually wears in a knot on top of her head. She has a dog called Wag and a cat called Lightfoot, and she lives in an upside-down house.

All the children love Mrs. Piggle-Wiggle, and Mrs. Piggle-Wiggle loves them. She is always ready to stop whatever she is doing and have a tea party, and she is glad to have children dig worms in her petunia bed. In fact, Mrs. Piggle-Wiggle just naturally understands children, which is of course why all the parents call Mrs. Piggle-Wiggle whenever their children are being difficult. Mrs. Piggle-Wiggle always knows exactly what to do to help cure children's bad habits, like not taking a bath, which was Patsy Brown's bad habit.

Up to the time of this story Patsy was just an everyday little girl. BUT ONE MORNING Patsy's mother filled the bathtub with nice warm water and called to Patsy to come and take her bath. But when Patsy saw the nice warm tub of water, she began to scream and yell and kick and howl like a wild animal.

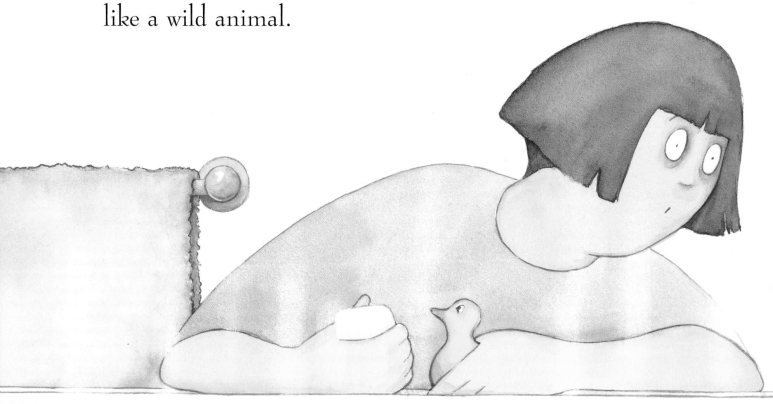

*N*aturally her mother was quite surprised to see her little girl acting so peculiarly, but she just said, "Now, Patsy, stop all this nonsense and hop into the tub."

Patsy ran from the bathroom, yelling, "I won't take a bath! I won't ever take a bath! I hate baths! I HATE BATHS. I haaaaaaaaaaaaate baaaaaaaaths!"

Patsy's mother let the water out of the tub and went downstairs to telephone Mrs. Piggle-Wiggle. She said, "Hello, Mrs. Piggle-Wiggle. This is Patsy's mother and I am having such a time this morning. Patsy simply will not take a bath."

Mrs. Piggle-Wiggle said, "I would say the Radish Cure is probably the quickest and most lasting. All you have to do is buy one package of radish seeds. Then let Patsy alone as far as washing is concerned. When she has about half an inch of rich black dirt all over her, scatter radish seeds on her arms and head. Press them in gently and then just wait."

The next morning Patsy's mother didn't say one single word to Patsy about a bath, and so Patsy was sweet and didn't act like a wild animal. The next day was the same and so was the next.

When Sunday came, Patsy was a rather dark blackish gray color, so her mother suggested that she stay home from Sunday school.

At the end of the third week Patsy skipped out to get the mail, and the postman, on seeing her straggly, uncombed, dust-caked hair and the layer of dirt on her face, neck, and arms, gave a terrified yell and fell off the porch.

Patsy's parents decided to keep Patsy indoors all the time after that, but Patsy seemed quite happy. Of course, it was getting hard to tell how she felt as her face was so caked with dirt that she couldn't smile and she talked "oike is—I am Atsy and I on't ake a ath." She also had to take little teeny bites of food because she couldn't open her mouth more than a crack.

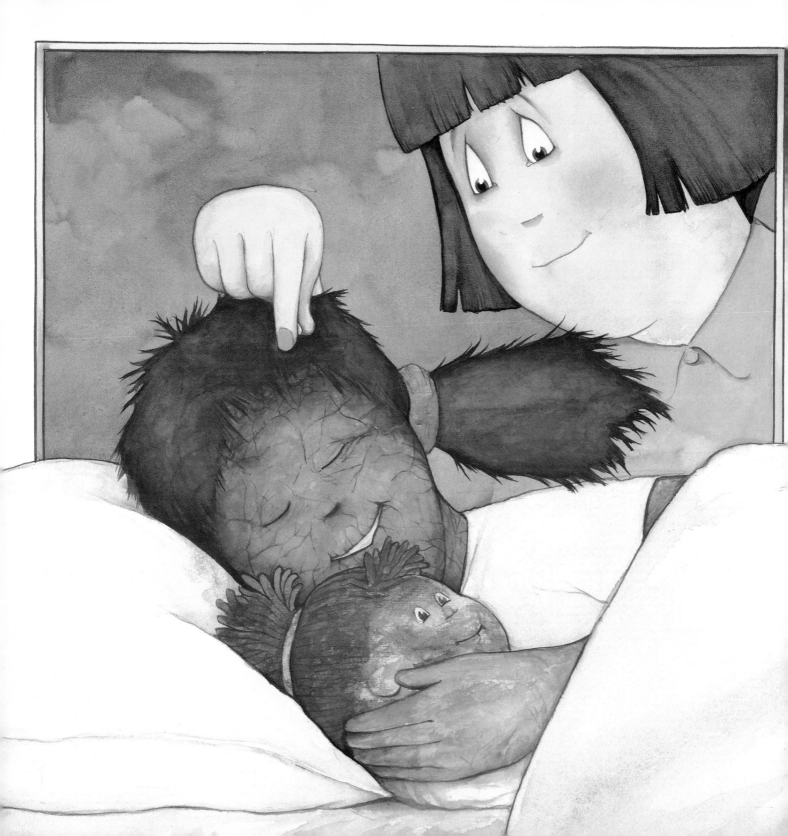

At last the day came when Patsy was ready to plant. That night when she was asleep, her mother and father tiptoed into her room and very gently pressed radish seeds into the dirt on her forehead, her arms, and the backs of her hands.

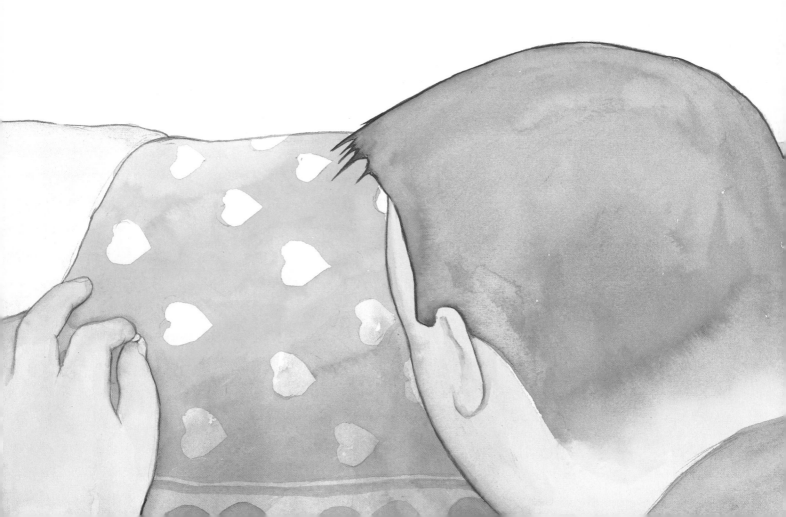

$\mathcal{S}$ome days later Patsy woke up one morning, and there on the backs of her hands and on her arms and on her forehead were GREEN LEAVES!

She jumped out of bed and ran down the stairs to the dining room, where her mother and father were eating breakfast. "Ook, ook at y ands!" she squeaked.

Her mother went over to Patsy, took a firm hold of one of the plants on her forehead, and gave it a quick pull. Patsy squeaked again, and her mother showed her the little red radish she had pulled.

Patsy suddenly said, "Other, I ant a ath!"

"What did you say, dear?" asked her mother, busily pulling the radishes and putting them in neat little piles on the dining room table.

"I oowant a b . . . b . . . ath!" said Patsy so plainly that it cracked the mud on her left cheek.

Patsy's mother said, "I think it had better be a shower," and without another word she went upstairs and turned on the warm water.

atsy was in the shower all that day. She used up two whole bars of soap, and she didn't even come out for lunch. But when her father came home for dinner, there she was, waiting for him at the door, clean and smiling, and in her hand she had a plate of little red radishes.